Flora

and the Flying Unicorns

Merry Christmas, Danielle

Hope your new year is filled with many happy memories and maybe a few magic unicorns!

your friend,
Sandy Watson 1991

Fiona

and the Flying Unicorns

Sandy Watson

Orca Book Publishers

Copyright © 1991 Sandy Watson

All rights reserved. No part of this book may be rerproduced in any form by any means without the written permission of the publisher, except by a reviewer who may quote passages in review.

Canadian Cataloguing in Publication Data
Watson, Sandy, 1945–
Fiona and the flying unicorns

ISBN 0-920501-68-0
I. Title.
PS8595.A87F5 1991   jC813'.54   C91-091541-5
PZ7.W37Fi 1991

Publication assistance provided by the Canada Council.

Orca Book Publishers
P.O. Box 5626, Stn. B
Victoria, B.C. V8R 6S4

Printed and bound in Canada

Illustrations by Terry Stafford

This book is dedicated to Mernie and to Grandad Haggith whose loving memories I still cherish;

to my parents, Joan and Jack Blair, for helping me grow up in a world of innocence and home-made fun;

to Patrick and Heather whose imagination and sense of wonder allowed me to rekindle my childhood joys all over again;

and to Bob, who found the strong, independent spirit inside me and set it free.

One

Fiona Malloy was in trouble again. She felt like a scarecrow dive-bombed by a flock of black birds. Feelings of guilt poked and pecked away at her conscience until she could stand it no longer.

"Daddy?" she heard her own voice sort of squeak.

Reverend Malloy locked the huge oak doors of the church, slipped the key into the pocket of his overcoat, then swept into a deep bow. "At your service, Milady."

Every Wednesday evening after choir

practise, her father played the same game, leading her by the hand down the steps of the Friends in the Valley Church as if she were a royal princess. But tonight Fiona did not feel like a princess. Her long blonde ponytails drooped like sagging ropes as she stared absent-mindedly at the buttons of her coat. One hour of practising with the children's choir usually left her happy and humming, but tonight, Fiona's heart felt as cold as the March wind.

"Tell me the truth, Daddy. Do you think Mom will still be mad at me?"

The glow from a street lamp cast two long shadows as Fiona's father cupped his hand under her dimpled chin. "Mad at you! Who could stay mad at this little mug." He gave her a wink, then took her hand and started walking towards the park. "I have a hunch that your mother will be waiting at home with a big bear hug and a cup of hot chocolate."

Fiona shook her head and kicked at a twig that had blown onto the sidewalk. "You didn't see her eyebrows scrunch up tight and her lip curl sideways at me this afternoon at the Brownie meeting," she explained with a frown. "I know I didn't exactly hand in the neatest sewing project in the world, but you have to admit mine WAS different from all the rest. Shouldn't I at least get points for coming up with a new idea?" As they strode past the post office, Fiona shivered and hunched up her shoulders against the wind.

Her father slowed his pace a little and said in a quiet, steady tone, "Oh your idea was creative, all right. No doubt about that, but you did not do what you were asked."

When they reached the intersection they stopped and waited for the WALK signal. Reverend Malloy looked down at his daughter and thought for a moment. Finally he spoke.

"Try to imagine how your mother felt. She volunteered four hours of her time to teach your Brownie pack how to sew, and on the day of the test, you show up, not with badges that have been neatly sewn, but with badges that have been STAPLED onto your uniform. I don't blame her for feeling embarrassed. I would have strung you up by your shoelaces!"

"But Daddy . . . "

"Oh no you don't," he interrupted with a grin. "Never mind that old BUT DADDY routine. This time your mother was right. You didn't plan your project ahead of time and you didn't follow the guidelines. Serves you right for dreaming up such a hair-brained last-minute scheme."

Fiona knew she was wrong. She chewed on her bottom lip, took a deep breath, and looked up into his eyes. "Think it would help if I tell Mom I'm sorry?"

"That's a good start, Pumpkin," said her father, taking her hands in his. "But I think what she really wants is a promise that you'll start planning your time more carefully and do what you're told when you're told to do it."

He squatted down and pointed at the stars twinkling in the night sky. "Remember how we used to lie on the lawn on summer nights and look for animal shapes in the stars and pretend there were magic unicorns up there racing by the light of the moon?"

Fiona gazed up at the Big Dipper and a smile spread over her face. "I still do that every night before bed," she murmured.

"Well, maybe that's part of our trouble," her father said kindly. "Sometimes I think that imagination of yours just lifts you up and carries you away." He put his arm around her shoulders and hugged her closer. "You're almost ten years old now, Fin. It's time to put away some of those daydreams and learn how to plan ahead. The secret is to find a happy balance. Think you can work on that, Princess?"

Fiona loved the way her soft-spoken father always gentled her around to his way of thinking. Her arms crept round his neck and she whispered, "How about I promise I'll try harder to follow the rules, if you promise to let the children's choir sing the song about Noah and the unicorns in church next Sunday. Ugga mugga?"

Her father kissed her on the end of the nose and repeated their secret code word. "Ugga Mugga," he replied cheerfully. Then he pawed the ground like an impatient horse at the starting gate. "Ladies and Gentlemen, they're at the post . . . the old war horse and the silver white unicorn. It's the race of the century. On your mark, get set, go!"

Reverend Malloy broke into a run, puffing and panting down Shannon Avenue under the weight of his bulky winter coat. As the old war horse galloped below the branches of the ancient chestnut tree, a magical, mystical unicorn named Fiona whinnied exuberantly and dashed past him to cross the finish line first.

The next day at school, it didn't take long for Fiona to drift off again into technicolour daydreams of graceful unicorns.

While the students in Room 4B cleared their desks after Art period, Miss Biolo's booming

voice echoed over the public address system at Cloverdale Elementary School. "And that concludes your closing announcements for Friday, March 22. Would Bradley Newcomb and Fiona Malloy please report to the office before leaving school? Have a good weekend, boys and girls."

Here we go again, thought Fiona, as she stared at the loudspeaker above the classroom door. I'll bet it's Mom phoning the school secretary to tell me she's stuck in a parish meeting and won't be home until four. Fiona beckoned to Taralin and began to put her art supplies away in her desk.

Like a hive of bees, the twenty-four other students in Miss Sawchuck's class buzzed around in a fast-motion frenzy, stuffing homework into book bags and backpacks, grabbing jackets and zooming out the door. Amidst the confusion, a yellow paper airplane careened across the room and crashed into the blackboard.

Newcomb the Nuisance! Fiona shook her head in disgust. Somewhere in the world there might be a species of life lower than Bradley Newcomb, but Fiona thought it was highly unlikely. She watched him pull a long string of gum from his mouth, stretch it out and drape it like a sticky spider web over the empty desk next to his. He pushed his bottom lip out, blew a fringe of frizzy red hair off his forehead and ripped another page from his scribbler. It was amazing how a cranky creep like Bradley could create such intricate aviation designs just by folding a simple piece of paper. But that was all he did all day.

This was Bradley's second year in Grade Four, and as Miss Sawchuck was so fond of saying, unless he could come up with a more intelligent answer than his standard "I dunno," his after-school detention total would go down in *The Guiness Book of World Records*.

When Bradley heard his name over the speaker, he grimaced and pressed harder on the crease he was folding. He hummed loudly as if to drown out the words, then held his latest paper masterpiece up to the light. He looked around. Miss Sawchuck was in the cloak room helping Joanne search for a lost gym sock. The classroom was almost empty, except for Fiona Malloy and Taralin Wong. Bradley made the sound of an aircraft engine ready for take-off. Six seconds later, a high-flying Newcomb Special glided over Fiona's head, circled once and came in for a perfect landing on the purple bow of her left ponytail.

"Bradleeee!" she squealed, shaking the paper plane from her hair. "You almost made me wreck my project!" Carefully she slid a long shimmering cylinder into a big plastic bag, so she wouldn't knock off any glitter from the pointy end where the freshly glued silver sparkles were still wet.

Taralin stuck out her tongue at Bradley, then whispered into the ear of her best friend, "See? I told you the principal would find out."

"Hush up," Fiona replied. She adjusted her ponytail ribbons and shot Bradley a dirty look.

Both girls glared as the boy drew back his arm and another paper plane took to the air, this time homing in on the wastebasket in front of Miss Sawchuck's desk. "All right!" he exclaimed, as his mission hit the target. "Two Pointer!"

Taralin sighed impatiently, then turned to pull Fiona closer. "If Mr. Johnson asks, promise me you'll tell him I only OPENED the study hall cabinet. Remember, YOU were the one who put the Barbie doll ballet skirt on the Boys Sports Trophy."

Fiona rolled her eyes and made a face. "Relax, Tara. It's probably just my mom leaving me a message to go to your place after school, because she's going to be late getting home from a meeting or something. C'mon, you can wait for me in the hall."

But as she sat on the hard-backed chair in

front of Mr. Johnson's giant oak desk, Fiona didn't feel quite so sure of herself. Why had Miss Biolo told her AND Bradley to wait in the office together?

Out the corner of her eye, Fiona watched Bradley crack his gum and pick at a scab on his elbow. Suddenly the sound of a high-flying jet reverberated against the outside window. Bradley leaned over and arched his neck to catch a glimpse of the graceful wings just before the plane banked into a billowy cloud.

The office door opened and Mr. Johnson strode in studying a list on a blue sheet of paper. He sat down behind his desk and peered over his wire-rimmed glasses at the two children. "Mr. Newcomb. Miss Malloy," he began. "Perhaps you can enlighten me as to why you two are the only students in Division Four who have not yet handed in plans for your Science Fair projects?" He paused, then arched his bushy eyebrows. "Well?"

Bradley looked as if he was lost in his own private world, examining the dust particles floating in through the window on a shaft of sunlight, so Fiona straightened her shoulders and spoke up with pride. "Actually Mr. Johnson, I don't even NEED a plan, because my project's coming along so well, but thanks very much for asking." She grinned and held up her plastic bag with the shimmering pointed cylinder inside.

"You see, I'm making this costume with silvery sparkles all over it. Wait till everyone sees me stand up in front of those judges all dressed up as . . . you'll never guess . . . " She raised her eyebrows and flashed him a happy grin. " The Queen of the Unicorns! Of course, I'm also writing a poem to read that explains how the great unicorns became extinct. Do you want to hear what I've got so far?"

Fiona reached into her bag and pulled out a scrap of note paper she had snitched from her father's phone message pad. She turned it right side up, cleared her throat and began to read the words she had so lovingly written:

"Where Did the Unicorns Go?
by
Fiona L. Malloy

Once long ago in a land faraway
A wonderful legend was born
A galloping, shimmering, mythical beast
With a beautiful bright golden horn
"What a graceful and magical creature
you are,"
Said a twinkling and winking night star

"And, well . . . that's all I've written so far, but I'll have it finished on time, don't you worry, Mr. Johnson."

Fiona beamed with joy at her splendid poem and folded her hands in her lap to wait for the principal's praise. She glanced toward the window and caught a glimpse of Bradley as he covered his mouth to smother a snicker.

Mr. Johnson saw it too and shot a stern look in Bradley's direction. "At least Miss Malloy has exercised her intellectual powers and come up with SOMETHING creative, which is more than I can say for you, sir!"

Fiona gave Bradley an "I told you so" look and settled back in her chair, comfortable at last.

The principal smiled weakly and shook his head. "Unfortunately, Miss Malloy, the existence of unicorns is based on fantasy, not scientific fact. I appreciate your efforts, but since the plight of the unicorns does not fit the official guidelines, you'll have to come up with another idea."

Fiona blinked twice. She gulped, unable to believe what she had just heard. Wistfully she imagined a majestic white unicorn standing alone on a windswept hilltop, silver teardrops cascading from its sad emerald-green eyes.

Mr. Johnson folded his arms and turned to Bradley. "Now, perhaps you'd be kind enough to dispose of that chewing gum, Mr. Newcomb, and tell us how your project is progressing."

Bradley spat out a wad of gum that clanged as it hit the bottom of the empty waste basket. He rocked back and forth on his chair, pulling the neck of his T-shirt until it stretched completely out of shape. He was obviously thinking hard about his answer.

Fiona heard the sound of the principal's fingers drumming impatiently on his desk and pictured her sad-eyed unicorn galloping off into the sunset.

"Still cogitating, I see," Mr. Johnson said with a scowl. "Well, young man, you'd better do more than just think about it. I expect to see the outline for a prize-winning Science Fair project on my desk first thing Monday morning. Do I make myself perfectly clear?"

Bradley scuffed at the floor and muttered something.

Slowly, Mr. Johnson rose from his chair. "I beg your pardon?"

"I said, I can do it, sir."

The principal smiled and reached out to shake his hand. "I KNOW you can do it, Bradley. Inside that thick skull of yours is a fine mind. Use it, boy!"

Mr. Johnson perched on the edge of his desk and turned his attention to the unicorn expert. "Now, Fiona, I want you to dream up a project that deals with FACTS, not fantasy. Get a copy of the guidelines from Miss Biolo on your way out. Remember this: If you haven't presented a plan by Monday morning, you'll both be assigned to the Animal Behaviour Team Project that Fiona's brother is heading up for Division Six. Well? See you both Monday morning."

Two

"Animal, vegetable, mineral . . . these topics all sound so boooring," Fiona whined as she flipped through the pages of the guidelines. It was too hard to read while she was walking, however, so she folded the two sheets and stuffed them into her pocket.

Taralin switched on a quizzical smile and wiggled her eyebrows. "Wanna come to my place and see something special?"

"You got ANOTHER new pet?" Fiona asked. She loved the strange menagerie at the Wong's farm. Taralin's parents kept a flock of white ducks, two parrots, three gerbils and a tank full of rainbow-coloured tropical fish. At Fiona's house, animals were taboo. "I wish my dad wasn't allergic to everything under the sun."

Taralin agreed. "It IS rotten. If you could have any pet in the whole wide world, what would you choose?"

Fiona grinned and pointed to the silver unicorn painted on her purple sweatshirt.

As they rounded the corner on Shannon Avenue, a fat calico cat lay on the sidewalk stretching a paw and yawning in the afternoon sun.

"Fluffy!" Fiona exclaimed. "What are you doing out here? We'd better take her back, Taralin, or Mrs. Dregger will be looking all over for her again." Fiona groaned as she lifted the heavy ball of fluff and staggered down the sidewalk to her next door neighbours' house. "What a lump you are, Fluffy."

Taralin sank her fingers into the cat's soft fur. "She must weigh twenty pounds! What do they feed you, Fluff? Steak?"

"Snakes!" growled a small voice from above. The girls craned their necks up to see Fiona's four-year-old neighbour, who was perched in the chestnut tree.

Fiona scowled. "Stanley Dregger, you come

down from there this minute! Wait till your mother catches you."

The owner of the dimpled, gap-toothed grin beaming down at them was the spunky little tyke Fiona affectionately referred to as "the beast." Every Saturday afternoon, Mrs. Dregger paid her two dollars to amuse Stanley, who adored the make-believe games Fiona created just for him.

Today he sat straddling the lowest branch of the old tree wearing grass-stained overalls and his faded "I Love Gramma" sweater. Between his chubby fingers dangled a foot-long earthworm.

"Din'cha hear me?" he croaked. "Fluffy eats snakes . . . big scraggly snakes like this one." Suddenly he dropped the squiggling worm and hollered, "Bombs away!"

Silently the "snake" plopped onto the upturned face of the unsuspecting cat. With a shocked yowl, Fluffy leapt out of Fiona's arms and skittered for safety, knocking over three garbage cans in her escape.

The grubby little runt shinnied to the ground and straightened the flowered kitchen curtain that hung down his back. "I'm betendin' to be Superman," he said, sniffing at a bubble that drooped from his left nostril. "Wanna play?"

Taralin cringed. "Eew . . . look at his nose. Disgusting!"

"Stanley, don't wipe it on your slee . . . too late . . . yuck!" Fiona shuddered. "Just look at you. Grape juice mustache, hair like a rat's nest, shoes on the wrong feet, AND they're untied as usual. YOU are a walking disaster!"

She plunked him down on the sidewalk, lifted his left foot and retied the mud-spattered lace.

Stanley grumbled that it wasn't his fault, that he had been in a big hurry 'cause a dinosaur was chasing him. And anyway, Superman didn't need to worry about tripping over his shoelaces, 'cause he flew everywhere. And anyone who didn't know that wasn't so smart, even if they WERE nine and COULD tie shoes.

He fiddled with the end of Fiona's ponytail ribbons and repeated his question, "Wanna play Superheroes?"

Fiona's answer was interrupted by Stanley's mom who hurried out of her house wiping her hands with a dish towel. "Come on, Stanno. Time for your bath. Gramma will be here in an hour for dinner. Are we still on for tomorrow afternoon, Fiona?"

"Sure, Mrs. Dregger. Mom says I can take him to the park. See you tomorrow, Stan."

An impatient Taralin pushed Fiona up the driveway past the mailbox that read "Reverend R.D. Malloy and Family." She dropped the pink backpack inside the kitchen door and yelled, "Fiona's at my place, Mrs. Malloy! We'll send her home in time for supper!" The girls bounded out back and across the field, then took the shortcut through the school yard to a small farm at the edge of town where Taralin's parents raised vegetables and bedding plants.

Here in the heart of the Fraser Valley, the outskirts of town and the open green space of the countryside were woven together like a daisy chain. Wild pheasants and field mice lived among the blackberry bushes that hugged the roadside ditches all the way to Mud Bay.

"Are you ready for the surprise?" asked Taralin, when they reached her back porch. Silently she opened the door and tiptoed down the hall.

After one step into her bedroom, Fiona squealed, "Babies! Your gerbil had babies! They're adorable."

The tiny gerbils nestled among the sawdust chips in the corner of their cage, curled up like sand-coloured powder puffs with long beige tails. As Fiona inched closer she giggled and hugged herself. Five little pink noses twitched and tried to burrow closer under their sleeping mother, whose gossamer-thin whiskers fluttered like fairy wings.

Taralin made little cooing noises and pointed with both index fingers. "Look at their tiny paws. Aren't they sweet?"

Skittering through a cardboard tunnel in the next cage was the gerbil father, his big brown eyes seemed to shine with pride. "Atta boy, Herman," Fiona said.

Mrs. Wong's voice called out from the adjoining bedroom which had been converted into a small office. "Taralin?" Her mother sat hunched over a pile of bills and ledger books. With a pencil clenched in her teeth, she pushed rows of beads back and forth on an abacus. The Chinese counting machine clicked as the red wooden beads bumped each other with every flick of her fingers.

"It's just me and Fin, Ma."

Mrs. Wong glanced up with a thin smile and waved hello. "Be right with you," she answered, jotting down one more number at the bottom of a column of figures. She tucked a strand of fine black hair behind her ear, then propped her elbow on the desk and rested her chin on the palm of her hand. Taralin did exactly the same thing at school every time she struggled over an arithmetic problem.

The girls wandered into the kitchen for an after-school snack. Taralin reached out to slide the cookie jar over from the back corner of the counter and whispered softly to her friend. "Things aren't so good this spring." She lifted the cookie jar lid, peeked inside and shook her head over the empty vessel. "My parents made a contract to sell apples for Banducci Orchards, but ever since the county work crew tore up the road, no cars have driven by, so . . . . " She raised her hands, palms up. "No customers, no sales."

Mrs. Wong's voice rang out from behind them. "And no cookies either, right? How about a slice of apple or a couple of carrot sticks?" She opened the refrigerator and passed them a jug of milk and a plate of fresh fruit and vegetable slices, then perched on a stool and rubbed her stiff neck.

"Grandfather liked to quote old Chinese proverb: *Patience is a necessary virtue.* Now I understand." She smiled and poured three glasses of milk. "Well, road will be finished soon. Signs point to good fortune."

"I wish the signs would point me in the direction of a new science project," said Fiona after a sip of milk. "Remember my Queen of the Unicorns idea?" Mrs. Wong nodded her head and chomped on a carrot stick. Fiona pointed both thumbs to the floor, stuck out her tongue and blew. "If I don't come up with a new plan by Monday morning, I'll be stuck with my know-it-all brother and his team of Grade Sixers researching the effects of diet and exercise on aging rabbits. Booorrring."

"Hey, wait a minute," exclaimed Taralin, wiping away a milk mustache. "Why not take home Herman? Design your own animal research project about gerbil fathers and how they act around their babies."

Fiona munched on her carrot and thought carefully. "I don't know. Everett only got permission to do his study on rabbits when he promised to build the hutch in the far corner of the backyard, 'cause of Dad's allergies."

"Weather nice enough for gerbil to stay in garage," suggested Mrs. Wong. "Try it for one, maybe two nights. If no good, bring Herman back. We help you find another idea."

At four-thirty that same afternoon, Fiona Malloy could be seen walking home talking to a little bump under the front of her sweatshirt.

"Wait till you see the project I'm planning

for you, Herman, old boy. Hey, hold still, will ya?" She nestled him deeper between her jacket and shirt and stepped over a slug on the side of the road. "I figure if I roll up a piece of foil, then tie it to your little forehead, you might look like a newborn baby unicorn."

Fiona reached her hand inside her jacket and tried to cuddle the fidgety creature, but every time she touched his soft warm fur, he nibbled nervously and burrowed back further around her middle and underneath her arm. "Quit wriggling, you little dickens," she said gleefully.

Just as Fiona cut across the school yard, a black Volkswagen sputtered and putt-putted in the parking lot. Mr. Johnson waved at her from behind the wheel and shifted gears. When Fiona raised her hand to wave back, Herman flicked his tail and tunnelled up into her sleeve and back down again sending her into a spasm of giggles. The principal looked puzzled as he drove past the jiggling, wiggling girl.

"Uh oh. What am I saying?" Fiona wondered aloud. "Mr. Johnson will never approve of ANY idea with unicorns in it. C'mon Herman, we'd better put on our thinking caps and start again."

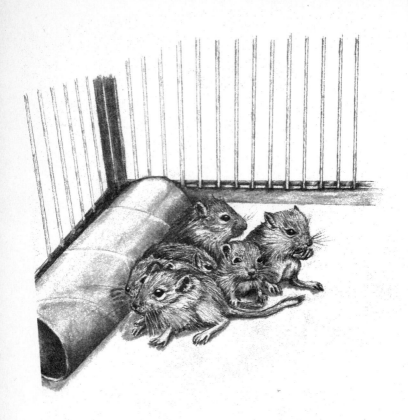

Three

Fiona opened her front door and listened before stepping inside. "Good. Mom's in the kitchen with the radio on," she murmured, as she listened to her mother crooning happily. "Now, not a peep out of you, Herman, until I find a shoe box, then I'll put you out in the garage."

She sneaked down the hallway to her bedroom at the back of the house. "Hmmn," she wondered. "Where can I put you till I find that box?"

She scanned the room searching for a

suitable hiding place. On the white chest of drawers was a glass box shaped like a hexagon where Fiona kept her hair ribbons. Nope. It would be too easy to spot Herman's beige fur amongst all the pretty coloured ribbons in that see-through box.

High above her unicorn poster was a string hammock where her stuffed animal collection lived. Fiona held her little friend up so they could both study the netting. "Not a good idea," she reasoned. "You'd slip right through those big holes and kerplop down on my head in the middle of the night, wouldn't you, you little rascal."

She cupped her hands together and watched Herman sit up on his hind legs and raise his front paws as if he was saying a prayer. Fiona chuckled. "Yes. I wish we could hurry up and find a hiding place, too."

Fiona kneeled on her braided rug and slid open the bottom dresser drawer where she kept her diary and other secret stuff, like the eagle feather she had found at Crescent Beach. She deposited the gerbil in the drawer, then turned to rummage through the pile of junk on the floor of her closet. All of a sudden, her ears picked out the sound of footsteps coming from the kitchen. "Oh no! It's Mom."

Fiona knew the rule: No animals in the house. She had only brought the gerbil in for a moment, but who would believe that! "Sssh," she said to her furry friend as she slid the bottom drawer half closed and turned to greet her mother, who poked her smiling face around the corner of the bedroom doorway.

"Thought I heard someone come home. Were you trying to sneak in without giving your Momma Bear a hug?" asked Mrs. Malloy, as she waltzed into the room with a pot holder in one hand and a wooden spoon in the other. Fiona guessed by the flour stains on her mother's apron and her glowing pink cheeks that she had been baking bread all afternoon, but the red smudge dribbling down her blue sweater and pants meant they were having something for dinner with tomato sauce on it.

Baby Bear stood up, wrapped her arms around Momma Bear and felt soothed by her warmth. They rocked back and forth for a moment feeling cuddly and cosy and loved. "Good news, Finny Minny," Mother said. "I had a call from Brown Owl this morning, and she says you can try your sewing test again next week. What do you think? Will you be ready this time?"

"Umn hmn. I promised Daddy I'd try

harder to plan ahead and follow every single rule in the boo . . . holy cow!"

Fiona's eyes darted to the dresser drawer where Herman was hiding. Two furry brown ears twitched from behind a pile of Sunday School papers in the left-hand corner of the drawer. Suddenly the gerbil rose on his hind legs and scratched at his little white belly. Fiona jumped, then dragged her mother by the hand out of the bedroom and down the long hallway toward the kitchen. "Um, I, uh, do I smell something burning?" Her mother sniffed the air and hurried into the kitchen to investigate while Fiona followed her, after pulling her bedroom door closed to conceal the scene of the crime.

Back in the kitchen, Mrs. Malloy dumped a fresh tray of hot buns into the bread basket and turned down the radio. The silence made Fiona nervous, so she tried to cover her guilt by humming and bustling about noisily gathering the knives, forks, plates and glasses and arranging them on the checkered tablecloth.

"Anybody home?" sang out Reverend Malloy from the front hall.

"Daddy!" Fiona ran to the front door and flew into his arms.

"Hello, Princess. How was . . . aaa . . . aaachoo!"

"Bless you!" called Mrs. Malloy from the kitchen. "We're out here slaving over a hot stove just waiting for some handsome prince to come and rescue us!"

Fiona's father laughed and dropped the evening paper beside the living room chair. Then he followed his nose towards the aroma that wafted from the kitchen. "MMMMmmmmm. And lasagna, too!" he exclaimed, as he peeked into the oven. He wrapped his arms around his wife and planted a noisy kiss on her cheek. "Anyone ever tell you, you're the best cook in the Fraser Valley?" Mrs. Malloy flashed a big smile and brushed a wisp of blonde hair from her eyes with her wrist.

A noise like a thundering herd of elephants echoed in the hallway, as a husky twelve-year-old wearing black cords and a T-shirt that said "$E=MC^2$" pounded down the stairs, slid across the waxed kitchen floor and screeched to a halt in front of the table. "Hi, Dad."

Reverend Malloy ruffled his son's sandy-coloured hair and pointed to the evening paper. "Well, Everett, did you hear?

The Canucks scored in overtime last night. What do you think of my team now?"

Everett threw a leg over his chair and pulled a miniature computer from his back pocket. "According to my calculations," he announced matter-of-factly, "that makes their chances of winning this year's Stanley Cup precisely . . . eleven to one."

Fiona rolled her eyes. Everett figured everything on the entire planet could be reduced to mathematical equations and little-known scientific facts. Fiona took the margarine from the fridge and grabbed the pitcher of milk.

"OK Einstein," she said impatiently. "Could you cut the number crunching long enough to put the bread basket on the table?"

Reverend Malloy's nose twitched. He wiggled it and took a deep breath. "Were you dusting today, dear?" he asked his wife.

Mrs. Malloy was too busy balancing the hot casserole dish to answer. As she spooned lasagna onto the plates, the family settled in their seats, then joined hands and said grace. Fiona silently added a little prayer of her own, then opened her eyes to the sight of her brother slathering margarine on his roll. He took a huge bite and smacked his lips in approval.

"Well," Everett declared after swallowing, "you'll be happy to hear that my Science Fair project plan has been officially approved."

Big mouth! thought Fiona, seething with irritation. Why did he have to bring up this stupid topic? She nibbled anxiously on a corner of her freshly baked bun. Dear Lord, she prayed in silence, don't let him snitch about me going to the principal's office.

"You must feel pleased after all those hours at the computer planning your experiments," said his mother.

"Well done," said his dad.

Fiona looked her smart-aleck brother square in the eye and made a fish face, blowing air into her cheeks and crossing her eyes.

"What's the matter, Fifi?" Everett said with a smirk. "Guilty conscience?"

"Any chance you two can get through an entire meal without bickering?" asked Dad, whose eyes were beginning to look red and puffy. "Now who's going to tell me what's going on?"

Fiona stabbed at her lasagna with murder on her mind.

Everett silently swallowed what was in his mouth, then grinned like a Cheshire cat and dropped the bomb. "Well, you'll find out on Monday anyway. Mr. Johnson told me he's assigning Fiona to work on my project. It seems she couldn't come up with a plan for the Science Fair that would meet the guidelines, so . . . . " He shrugged his shoulders and spoke to his parents in a grown-up voice as if his sister wasn't even in the room. "Maybe next time she'll remember to follow the rules."

Fiona fumed. She pictured Everett standing nervously in front of a tree as she pulled a toilet plunger from her imaginary quiver, placed it in her bow and shot it through the air. She gritted her teeth as she imagined the plunger hitting him smack in the middle of his face, closing those flapping lips forever within the smelly circle of a rubber suction cup.

Reverend Malloy squeezed his eyes shut and wiggled his nose three times in rapid succession. He stretched his mouth into strange contortions, but it was too late. "A . . . aah . . . " He grabbed a table napkin just in time to smother the explosion. "Aachooo!"

"Bless you again!" clucked Mrs. Malloy like a mother hen. "I wonder if you're coming down with the same flu that Alice Reener had. She says half the choir was laid low. Time to cook up a big pot of my famous chicken soup I guess."

Everett smiled like an angel and said in a syrupy sweet voice, "Voulez vous passer moi du lait, ma petite soeur? Hey, what happened to your sweatshirt? Looks like something Stanley's cat dragged in."

Reverend Malloy sneezed again . . . and again.

Fiona shifted uncomfortably in her chair and shot her brother a hateful look.

One by one Everett counted, pointing out eleven holes in Fiona's shirt, right in the spot where Herman had been curled up in a ball, nibbling and chewing.

Reverend Malloy wiped his red nose. Mrs. Malloy's eyes darted from left to right. She put down her fork, and as Reverend Malloy sneezed again, she handed him a box of tissues from the corner of the counter. Fiona watched her mother's brow furrow as she began to put two and two together.

Suddenly Mrs. Malloy held up her hand. "Sssshh! I could have sworn I heard something. Listen!" She slid her chair away from the table, stood up, listened, frowned again and followed the scratching sound down the hall towards the back of the house.

It didn't take long before her stern voice echoed back down the hallway from her daughter's bedroom. "Fiona Leannder Malloy!

33

I want to speak to you . . . right this minute, young lady."

Fiona trudged down the hall, desperately trying to think of a good excuse for disobeying the house rules. When she stepped through her bedroom doorway, she saw Mother, both fists on her hips, glaring first at Fiona and then at the open bottom drawer. There in a heap of tattered and torn bits of cardboard and paper was Herman, nibbling merrily.

"Perhaps you'd be good enough to explain what this rat-like animal is doing in your dresser drawer."

"It's . . . it's . . . " As Fiona moved closer she noticed the colour of the bits of gnawed paper strewn around under the gerbil's feet. "It's chewing the corner of my diary!" Fiona squealed in dismay. "Herman!"

"You are in BIG trouble, Missy," declared her mother as she stomped back into the kitchen.

While Father sneezed and dabbed at his watery eyes, Mom telephoned Mrs. Wong to ask if Herman would survive a night in the garage until he could be returned first thing in the morning.

Fifteen minutes later, Everett was still shaking his head in disbelief as he finished his turn at drying the dishes. Fiona returned from the garage where it had taken seven lullabyes and a lot of soft stroking before Herman had settled down to sleep on an old blanket in a cardboard box just inside the side door.

On her way back through the kitchen, Fiona dodged the dish towel her brother flicked in her direction and scowled. "Tattle tale!"

Everett glowered back. "Imbecile!" he replied with relish. He rolled the damp dish towel into a ball and threw it at her head, but Fiona ducked and escaped to safety behind the bathroom door. Her brother snickered and headed out the back way to go collecting from his newspaper subscribers.

Reverend Malloy sniffled, snuffled and disappeared into his study to work on Sunday's sermon. In the living room, Mrs. Malloy propped her feet up and paged through a cookbook for a soup recipe that would feed the fifty-five people she expected for Sunday's church supper.

Fiona was banished to her bedroom for disobeying the rule about no animals in the house. She lay back on her bed sighing and staring at the silver stars she had pinned to her ceiling. She fingered the ruffle on her eiderdown quilt and wondered if there was some special section in her brain marked TROUBLE where all her best ideas came from.

On her night table a small box glowed in the darkness. She reached over and wound the key. The tinkling notes of "Somewhere Over the Rainbow" filled the air and warmed her heart. Fiona hummed her favourite melody.

"That's where the unicorns have gone," she thought, "over the rainbow." She hugged herself, then rolled onto her side and heard a crinkling sound in her pocket. Fiona pulled out a folded piece of paper.

As she re-read the Science Fair guidelines and thought back to Mr. Johnson's warning, a scientific fact nudged its way into her mind.

"A gerbil can eat its way out of a cardboard box! What if Herman escapes and gets lost under the car? What if Fluffy finds him first?"

Fiona propped herself up on her elbow and stared out her bedroom window at the garage. She pictured Stanley's overweight cat slumped against her father's workbench, burping and picking bits of gerbil meat out of his teeth with a toothpick.

When Everett and her parents were finally in bed, Fiona tiptoed out back. The haunting sound of a train whistle echoed in the distance like an eerie monster. Fiona shivered and edged the garage door open an inch.

Suddenly something scurried over her

slippered foot and cowered beneath the ruffle of her nightie.

"Herman!" she gasped. "You almost gave me a heart attack!" She scooped him up, then dragged in the laundry hamper she had carried up from the basement.

"There," she whispered, nestling the furry pet on the soft pile of dirty clothes in the plastic hamper. She closed the lid and smiled with satisfaction. "You can't eat your way out of that!" she said triumphantly. The tiny animal, tired from the day's adventures, curled up in a ball and promptly went back to sleep.

"Not a bad idea if I do say so myself," Fiona mumbled with a yawn.

The next morning, before the rest of the family awakened, Fiona dressed quickly and slipped outside.

"Oh no . . . not again!" she exclaimed as she peeked under the lid of the laundry hamper. Judging by the holes in the layer of soiled clothes, it was easy to see that Herman had eaten a rather substantial midnight snack. "Eeew! How could you chew on Everett's smelly old gym socks?!"

Just as the gerbil sank his front teeth into the corner of one of Reverend Malloy's white collars, Fiona snatched him up and aimed her index finger at his tiny nose. "Grrr! I should put you in a pot and cook you for dinner! Now I'm REALLY in trouble!" From upstairs, she could hear the sound of her father's electric razer. "Oops. Better make a run for it!"

Fiona nestled the animal into the pouch pocket of her purple jogging suit, zipped up her quilted jacket and scampered off towards Taralin's house.

Four

As Fiona reached McLellan Road, she spied an orange truck flashing its warning light. Behind a wooden barrier, three workmen stood on the black asphalt admiring the straight yellow lines they had just painted down the middle of the fresh pavement. A man in an orange construction helmet leaned out the truck window and hollered, "How about a cup of java at the donut shop before we finish the crosswalk?"

"Sounds mighty good to me, Jack," said the short worker in the orange safety vest. He clapped the other two men on the back and climbed into the back of the truck.

"Honk. Honk," The driver tooted at Fiona as he drove the truck up on the sidewalk to get past the line of directional cones and around the DETOUR barrier with the flashing yellow arrow.

Fiona's eyes danced with excitement as she raced to the Wongs' house. "They're almost done!" she sang. By the time she reached the house and handed Herman over to Taralin, her good news came out in short gasping breaths.

"Guess what? I just . . . heard . . . the work crew . . . your road . . . it's almost finished. Now all you need to do is advertise . . . and you'll get all your customers back."

Mr. Wong looked up from the porch floor where he was tracing letters onto a big piece of cardboard. "We have no money for advertise, Fiona."

Taralin slipped Herman into the second of two cages that basked in the sunshine on the porch steps. She looked over her father's shoulder. "Papa, the English word for apple has two p's in it."

"Could I help?" Fiona asked. With a red felt pen she drew thick block letters, then decorated them with candy-cane stripes. In the top right-hand corner of the make-shift sign, she

40

drew a sun with a happy face. "There," she said pointing proudly, "that part tells people they'll get friendly service at Wong's."

The screen door swung open and Mrs. Wong stepped outside, pulling a warm sweater around her. "Very nice. Now we put up sign, hope for the best."

"The sign! That's it!" exclaimed Fiona. She threw the felt pen to Taralin and called out, "Write FREE GERBILS on that other piece of cardboard. I'll be right back."

Fiona dashed down the road to the intersection and dragged the DETOUR barrier from the middle of the street up onto the sidewalk. "There," she said to herself. "No one will see it up here out of the way." Then she turned the arrow sign so it pointed to Wong's farm and moved the red cones so they pointed straight to the driveway in front of the Wong's greenhouses.

A big white car slowed at the corner and Fiona waved a cheerful hello. She gestured for them to drive into the farmyard where an old hay wagon was stacked high with boxes of apples and the last of their fall crop of carrots and onions.

"Right this way, ladies and gentlemen, for the juiciest apples in Cloverdale Valley." She picked up a shiny apple and held it high like an Olympic torchbearer.

As the white car slowed to a halt in the yard, Fiona leapt up onto an overturned box in front of the hay wagon. Like a television game show hostess, she spun around and pointed to a sack of onions. "What am I bid for these championship onions, ladies and gents? Nothing like a pot of homemade onion soup to scare away those nasty germs this time of year!" Fiona reached for a giant onion and raised it and the apple aloft like two trophies.

Taralin held out her hand to help a lady in a fur coat from the big white car.

Fiona continued to spout like an actress up on her pedestal. "Here you go, Madame," she said graciously, offering the smiling lady a free sample. To Fiona's surprise, she discovered that she had offered the lady not the apple, but the onion. The lady's eyes twinkled merrily. She thanked Fiona politely, put both samples back and picked up a small basket of apples.

Meanwhile, as Taralin finished propping the FREE GERBILS sign up on the gatepost, a station wagon full of cub scouts slowed down and backed up into the farmyard. Eight young boys in uniform tumbled out, making a beeline for the gerbil cage. They squeezed together, peeked at the babies and asked when they'd be ready to leave the nest.

Mr. and Mrs. Wong beamed at their good fortune and offered Chinese sweets and fresh apple slices to everyone.

"Great place you have here," said the lady in the fur coat as she paid for a bag of carrots and the basket of apples. "And the service beats anything I've seen in years."

"Thank you," Mrs. Wong replied with a shy smile. "Hope you can come back soon when our spring flowers in bloom."

Mr. Wong lifted a bushel basket of apples into the station wagon, while the cub leader rounded up his troop.

As the big white car left, another

customer drove into the farmyard. "Beep, beep," Fiona's mother waved from behind the steering wheel of her blue mini-van. Fiona waved back and walked toward her to share the good news. Suddenly, Fiona noticed a strange trail of yellow behind the back wheels of her mother's vehicle.

Squinting into the spring sunshine, she retraced the yellow stains all the way back to the new road and gasped. The freshly painted, once-neat-and-tidy, yellow lines were now a maze of squiggley smudges!

"Oh no!" cried Fiona, clapping her hand over her mouth in disbelief. "Another good idea gone bad. I think I'm in trouble again."

And with that, she took off like a rocket for home.

Five

"It's hopeless," Fiona groaned as she watched Everett in the back yard pacing out the measurements for his rabbit hutch. "I'll never come up with a proper plan for a science project in time for Monday morning. All my ideas just get me into trouble." She finished her letter to the mayor (apologizing for the mess she'd made on the new road) and slipped it into an envelope.

"Bzzzt!" The sound of the back door buzzer drilled straight through her ear drums bristling the hairs on the back of her neck.

A bundle of energy in a flowered curtain cape charged into the kitchen and announced himself with a blast on his imaginary trumpet. "Ta daa! Soup-erman!"

"Take those muddy boots off at the door, Stanley."

The boy with the permanent grape juice mustache did as he was told for once, then slid across the waxed floor towards the kitchen table. "Yer s'posed ta take me to the park now, Fin."

He grabbed a cereal box left on the table from breakfast, tipped it up in the air, shook it and tried to catch the falling Cheerios in his open mouth. The score was:

Kitchen Floor: 157 / Superman: 3

Fiona surveyed the mess and snarled, "You have the brain of a caterpillar and the manners of a wart hog." She opened the cupboard and took out the broom and dust pan. Stanley picked at a blob of peanut butter smudged on his saggy blue jeans and grumbled, "Bossy old busy body." As Fiona swept, Stanley flicked a leaf from the sleeve of his sweater. Then his hand crept towards his runny nose.

"Stanley!" Fiona dropped her broom and

tried to grab his sleeve. Too late. The four-year-old stepped back, rolled his eyes and slapped himself on the forehead. "I nearly fergot ta feed Fluffy! See ya outside."

Fiona emptied the dust pan and put away the broom. Babysitting Stanley for a couple of hours wouldn't be so bad if she didn't have that stupid science project on her mind. She yanked her jacket off the hook, grabbed her scarf and pushed her feet into her white rubber boots. The back door swung open and Fiona stepped outside.

"Stanleee!" she called.

There he was, lying on his stomach on the sidewalk trying to stuff a worm into the cat's mouth.

Fiona took one look at Stanley's slimy upper lip and shuddered. Like a magician, she fished a tissue from the end of her sleeve with a flourish. "Abracadabra, ready, aim, blow!" she ordered. "Your nose drips like a garden hose."

"My mom maked us a picnic," he said, pointing to the hamper in the wagon. Fiona recognized the old wicker basket the Dreggers always took to the beach. Whatever treats were inside had been covered by what looked like a green rubber blanket folded over the top. "That's my dad's rain poncho to spread on the grass at the park."

"All set, then?" Fiona picked up the wagon handle.

Superman snapped her a salute. "Ready," he croaked.

Fiona took one giant step and bellowed, "Forward march! Hup one two, huppity hup one two." Superman and the Queen of the Unicorns tramped off on their adventure.

A cold March wind whistled through the chestnut tree as Fiona rolled along the sidewalk pulling Stanley in the wagon. Stanley sat with the picnic hamper between his legs, while he directed an imaginary marching band. They headed up the hill towards the park. Grey clouds loomed on the horizon. At the corner, they spotted Bradley Newcomb and his bratty brother Shane sitting on the curb crushing marbles with a rock.

Bradley's older brother rubbed his ear against the shoulder of his black leather bomber jacket and scratched at his thick red hair. Shane had a tough mean streak that made him the terror of the school. Hoping they wouldn't notice her, Fiona silently paraded past. No such luck.

The two bullies unfolded their long legs

and stood up, falling into step on each side of the wagon.

"Hey, Malloy, where d'ya think you're goin'?" barked Bradley.

"Mind your own business," Fiona answered.

"Aw, ain't that cute," sneered Shane, leaning down to pinch Stanley on the cheek. "She's takin' this little piggy to market."

Fiona chewed her lip and walked faster, hoping they couldn't hear the pounding of her heart. Bradley came up from behind and yanked hard on her ponytails. It hurt like the dickens, but Fiona bit her lip, stared straight ahead and kept walking, squeezing her temper so it wouldn't jump out.

Shane grabbed the end of the curtain around Stanley's neck and in a high, girlish voice called out, "What a pretty dress you're wearing, Sissy-face!" Stanley wrenched it back and growled.

Bradley cackled with laughter at his older brother's antics.

Shane lifted his big green boot and kicked it against the back rim of the wagon. "Stanley is a baabee, a little bitty baabee!" This time Shane shoved his foot harder, and the wagon bashed into the back of Fiona's legs.

Fiona felt like a cobra coiled and ready to strike. She spun around and lashed out at her

50

enemies. "Stop it right now!" Stanley's eyes widened as he sensed the poison in her voice.

Bradley threw his hands up. "Mercy me! I'm so scared!"

All the kids in the neighbourhood had been afraid of the Newcomb brothers since they moved in last summer, so Fiona chose her next words carefully. "We're not bothering you. Let us pass."

Bradley lunged to block her path. He folded his arms across his chest and shook his head. "No way."

Suddenly Shane reached into his pocket and pulled out a big rock. "We're gonna line you two up fer target practise," he snickered, narrowing his eyes like a wicked witch and pounding the rock into the palm of his dirty hand. Then he spat on the rock, tossed it up in the air and caught it again.

Something inside Fiona snapped. Before he knew what had happened, Fiona kicked the rock out of Shane's hand, yanked the handle of the wagon and dashed across the road into a nearby field.

As they hurtled over the bumpy ground, Stanley curled his lips inward, dumbfounded by the sudden turn of events. He held on for dear life, pressing his rubber boots hard against the front rim of the wagon as he bumped up and down.

Fiona bounded across the field, puffing from the weight of the awkward load she was pulling. On and on they thundered, ploughing over deep ruts, spewing clumps of dirt and billows of dust behind them. When she felt brave enough to sneak a look over her left shoulder to see if their enemies were gaining on them, Fiona heaved a sigh of relief. In the distance, she could see Shane's leather jacket and Bradley's tall bulky shape turning towards the park. She let the wagon roll to a halt and gasped, "Thank goodness. We're safe."

"That was too bumpy," Stanley whined, rubbing his backside. "My bum hurts."

One last ray of sunshine slipped behind the giant roll of grey clouds that had somehow swooped down on them. Stanley shivered and turned his back against the cold wind.

"Well, we're not going back the way we came, that's for sure," muttered Fiona, " . . . not with Bradley and Shane blocking that sidewalk."

Fiona looked for a gap in the fence that divided the field they were standing in from their neighbourhood. A thick tangle of blackberry bushes stretched for almost a mile.

"Darn," she said. The only way back is

to circle around through old man Banducci's orchard."

"Oh oh," said Stanley hesitantly. "If he catches us he'll skin us alive!"

Stanley was right, but there didn't seem to be any other choice. Fiona's foot began to tap anxiously as if it were controlled by some unseen force. "I have to think!" she said through clenched teeth.

A strong gust of wind whipped a roofing shingle past like a frisbee. Stanley pointed at Fiona and giggled. "Yer ponytails are flappin' in the wind like bird wings!" Fiona laughed and bent down to untangle the rain poncho from the picnic hamper. "Didja see I brung my Superman cape and these secret magic energy pills from the moon?" he chirped, unrolling his balled fingers to reveal a gritty palm full of old jujubes covered with fuzzy blue lint.

Fiona grinned and rubbed one cold ear. She looked up once more at the angry sky, then scrunched the poncho over Stanley's head, spreading the ends out to cover the hamper too. Above them, dark hammer-head clouds rumbled like kettle drums.

"Grizzly bears!" Stanley gasped, tucking his head between his shoulders. His eyebrows shot up like two boomerangs. "Let's betend we're goin' to hunt wild animals. I got my Batman flashlight, so I can jist shine it on them and it zaps 'em dead, OK?"

Fiona tugged on the handle of the wagon, dragging her passenger over the ploughed furrows of earth that slipped and crumbled under her boots. "I've got a better idea," Fiona shouted into the wind. "You can be a famous explorer hunting for the lost land of the unicorns."

The famous explorer wiped his nose on his sleeve as they trundled towards a wire fence with a high wooden gate. Fiona flipped the latch and pulled the wagon through the opening. Behind them, the gate slammed shut, then creaked open again in the wind.

"Now we're in the land of the evil Snake King and he looks just like old man Banducci," Fiona explained in a low voice. She'd teach Stanley not to scare girls with snakes and worms.

They rumbled down a long gravel lane, pretending the squeak of the wagon wheels was the sound of hyenas and monkeys.

"Let's say we're on a barge on the Congo River and the secret map is hidden in that picnic hamper. Keep a sharp lookout now!" Fiona speeded up her footsteps, but toned down her voice so the words sounded scarier.

"Watch out for the Snake People. They're covered in slime and hang from trees, glomping onto anyone who passes underneath."

Stanley scraped his top teeth over his bottom lip and clicked to make her hurry faster. "Giddyup, horsey. I don't know if I like this story," he muttered.

Fiona broke into a trot and yelled out, "Careful or the Snake King will snatch your eyeballs and make them into a necklace."

The wind wailed through the trees. Stanley squeezed his eyes shut. "Don't let them get me, will you, Fin?" he begged.

Suddenly two ice cold raindrops plopped onto Fiona's head. From the huge dark cloud ahead of them, lightning flashed and thunder boomed.

Fiona froze in her tracks.

The wagon lurched to an emergency stop. "Ow! You made me bite my tongue!" cried Stanley.

A second thunder clap cracked in their ears. "One Mississippi," Fiona whispered, counting the seconds between the sound of thunder and the flash of lightning. "Two Mississippi." How close were they to those dangerous forks of lightning?

Stanley peered up at her in confusion.

Fiona didn't know what to do next. Trying to look very brave, she began to hum.

Dead leaves and specks of dirt whipped against their faces. The wind howled and moaned. Another bolt of lightning shot down from a black cloud.

All at once the sky opened up, pelting them with hail stones that sounded like ricocheting bullets.

"Let's make a dash for Banducci's barn!" she cried. "Hang on, Stan!"

Fiona scampered toward the shelter. Bumping up and down behind her in the wagon, rode the little explorer with his hands locked over his head and his eyes wild with excitement.

Then, they saw him . . . charging down the lane like a wounded bull and bellowing in a rage. It was old man Banducci.

Six

Fiona and Stanley cowered under an apple tree beside the gravel lane while old man Banducci rubbed his bald head where the hail stones had pounded him. His rough clay-coloured skin looked like a two-week-old mushroom, all wizened up and spotted. He pulled out a navy bandana from the pocket of his faded overalls to wipe his wet face.

The hail had changed to rain, so things were getting better, but as soon as Mr. Banducci opened his mouth, Fiona knew things were going to get worse.

"Why alla time you kids wanna come my orchard, steal apples, leava gate open, chickens get out . . . you no see da sign?"

"But . . . but . . . but . . . " Fiona tried to interrupt so many times, she sounded like the engine of a motorboat.

The wind was blowing the rain sideways now, flipping the edge of Stanley's poncho so it kept flying up and smacking him on the back of the head. Banducci switched to barking in Italian and pounded his fist into his other weatherbeaten hand.

"Wait, please!" Fiona yelled over the noise of the storm. "If you'll just let me explain . . . "

Just then another problem wheeled into view. Everett pedalled up the gravel driveway and swerved to dodge the puddles that had quickly formed in the low spots. Heavy rain splashed down the side of his almost-empty newspaper bag.

"Oh no," groaned Fiona. "It's Mr. Potato Head. Now we're in for it when he snitches to Mom and Dad about this."

She knew she had to pipe up with her side of the story fast, so she interrupted the farmer's angry speech. Planting her hands on her hips, Fiona yelled, "Excuse me!" hoping Everett would remember to report her politeness. "We were just taking a shortcut when the storm hit, so we ran down here for cover." Fiona had to shout to be heard against the wind, the thunder and the rain.

Behind Banducci's back, she could see her drenching wet brother signalling for her to cool it. But Fiona wanted to set the record straight about everything. "And it was Bradley Newcomb and his bratty brother Shane who stole your apples and started that throwing war on Hallowe'en," she added. "It's just not fair blaming us."

While the cranky old man digested this information, Everett leaned forward and handed over a soggy copy of *The Surrey Leader*. "Here's your paper, sir. Sorry it's a little wet."

Mr. Banducci's suspicious eyes flicked over the three children as if they were escaping criminals.

Everett hitched up his trousers and spoke again. "I'll just collect my sister and we'll get out of your hair . . . oops," he winced with embarrassment as his eyes focused on the farmer's bald head, "I mean out of your way, and off your property."

Stanley swung his legs around to the side of the wagon and slid onto the rain-soaked grass. He tugged at the farmer's overalls and croaked, "Why you bein' such a old grump, Mister?"

Banducci narrowed his black eyes and wagged his finger menacingly. His voice bit out the mean, hard words. "Maybe I calla police — teach you a lesson."

Stanley glared up into the wrinkled scowling face. His little hands curled into fists. Then he hauled back his leg and kicked the frowning farmer right square in the shin.

The air was split by a string of angry Italian words!

That was enough for Stanley. He spun around and skedaddled through the trees in the driving rain, jumping over the sprinkler heads with his poncho flapping behind him like a sail.

Mr. Banducci was mad. He looked as if his eyeballs might pop right out of their sockets.

Everett's mouth hung open in surprise. "Stanley! Get back here and apologize!" he yelled. "I'll get him, sir." Then Everett let go of the handlebars of his bike to give chase. Fiona cringed as the metal fender of her brother's falling bicycle thudded against the old man's knee and scraped all the way down his other shin.

Mr. Banducci roared like a raging lion.

Next thing she knew, Fiona was leaping across the sprinklers too, yanking the wagon and the bouncing picnic hamper behind her, trying to put as much space as possible between her and Banducci, who was limping in a circle and cursing at the top of his lungs.

Everett zigged and zagged in and out of the rows of apple trees as he gained on Stanley, whose baggy jeans, giant poncho and floppy rubber boots slowed him down.

The little guy scooted through a hole in the fence. On the other side was a construction site where a new subdivision was being built. When Stanley turned to look behind him, he tripped, lost his balance and landed flat on his kisser in a huge puddle of mud. He struggled to his knees, wincing as the cold water seeped through his clothes and lapped halfway up to his waist.

By the time Fiona caught up to them, Everett was laughing so hard, he was holding his sides and gasping for breath.

Every time Stanley tried to stand up in the gooey mud, his footing gave way and he fell over again with an even bigger splash. Finally he gave in and sat up straight and tall, pleased to be the centre of so much attention.

"Hey, lookit me!" he chimed, slapping his hands in the dirty water. Then he scooped and splashed, held his face up to the steady rain and sang out joyfully, "I'm havin' a bath!"

Seven

Fiona and Everett couldn't stay mad at him for long. They had to think of a way to get him out of that giant pool of muddy water. But each time they tried to wade in to rescue him, their boots slipped in the slimy mud and threatened to dump them in too. The Malloy children huddled for a conference, shivering in the rain, with the wind whistling through their soggy clothes. How could they drag Stanley out of that filthy puddle?

"I'm betendin' I'm a duck," said the little

squirt in the green poncho. "Quackity quack quack."

Fiona had an idea. "Maybe we can find a rescue pole in that pile of junk the builders left over there by the fence." They kicked through the stack of rubble until Everett uncovered a long piece of wood that looked strong enough to fish out a forty pound duck.

"OK Fiona, just stay out of the way. This is man's work," her brother insisted. He grasped one end of the board and leaned out over the puddle to aim the other end at Stanley.

The little runt plunked his fingers on his end of the two-by-four like a piano player and waited for his orders.

"No, dummy!" Everett grunted. "Grab hold with both hands and when I pull you up, just hang on."

The board was so long it wobbled and wibbled, so Fiona rolled an empty oil drum on its side and Everett propped the middle of the long piece of wood over the barrel for balance.

"Hey, that's great, Fin! The barrel acts like a fulcrum, so the board becomes a teeter totter. Good thinking."

"Fulcrum, schmulcrum," snapped Fiona. "Just hurry up and get him out. I am freezing cold and totally soaked!"

The science whiz lowered his end of the board, slowly easing Stanley's end a little higher. "Now, try to stand up again, Stan . . . careful! Lean over the board with your stomach . . . good. Just hang on tight till I swing you out of the puddle."

Everett slowly took the weight of the stocky four-year-old, who was now hanging in mid-air over the mud hole. Suddenly two little legs started kicking with delight. "Hey, lookit me! I'm flyin'!" Stanley shouted. "I'm Superman!"

With all that wiggling and kicking on the raised end of the board, Everett had to wrestle to keep his balance at the other end. If only they could keep Stanley hanging on in the air until they could swing him clear of the water.

"Woooops!" Everett wobbled backwards, lost his footing for a second and stumbled on a piece of plywood that slanted down from the nearby scrap pile. Fiona lunged forward and hooked her arms around his broad middle to steady him. Together, they swung the bobbing rescue pole up and over until they had safely deposited their dripping wet friend on the ground.

"Hurray!" they cheered, patting each other on the back and slapping hands like a winning baseball team as the rain plastered their hair to their heads.

Stanley scrambled to his feet and licked a river of water that had trickled off the end of his nose. "That was fun. Let's do it again!"

The corner of Everett's mouth curved upwards in half a smile. He grabbed his heart as if he was going to faint and shook his head. "Never again!" he cried.

Stanley and Fiona got the giggles while Everett played the part of a dying cowboy. He staggered around in the mud, and groaned like the world's greatest actor. Suddenly, the side of the lumber pile shifted and pieces of wood and wallboard tumbled down as if there had been an earthquake.

A piercing scream ripped through the air.

One look at Everett told Fiona he wasn't kidding any more. Something was terribly wrong. He had fallen on his back and his face was twisted in pain.

"My . . . foot," Everett gulped. "I can't move . . . my foot." His left leg was pinned under a pile of debris.

Fiona's head began to spin. She closed her eyes and took one long deep breath. Her stomach tensed in a knot, but she knew she had to act fast. Fiona bent in front of her brother, cleared away two big boards, then grabbed both sides of a huge piece of wallboard. But no matter how hard she tried, she could barely budge it. "It's too heavy!" she groaned. "Stanley, come and help me. Quick!"

Through clenched teeth, Everett sobbed and shook out three whispered words, "Get it . . . off!"

"OK Ev," she ordered, "close your eyes and count to three."

On "One," Fiona tightened her grasp, signalled Stanley with her eyes and chewed the inside of her lip. On "Two," she wedged her knee under the drywall for leverage and took a deep breath. By "Three," they had heaved the wallboard up and pushed it away.

"You OK?" Fiona crouched down to check, but one look at Everett's foot told her he was not. Her brother's face and leg looked far too white. The skin above his ankle was badly scraped, and his foot hung limp and twisted.

He shuddered, grabbed her arm, and tried to mouth the correct words. "Feels . . . like it's broken."

"Stanley, bring the wagon! We've got to get that foot out of the mud. Here, Ev. Lean on me and I'll help you up."

Fiona didn't know what to do, but she figured they would never be able to drag

Everett all the way home in the wagon. He was just too heavy in all that mud. She squinted through the rain towards Banducci's orchard where her brother had left his bicycle. No chance. They could never go back for the bike with Banducci on the prowl.

"Hey, Ebret, how come yer face is all grey?" asked Stanley. Sure enough, Everett had begun to shiver uncontrollably and the remaining colour had drained from his cheeks.

"I think I'm gonna throw up," he said shakily.

"You are not!" Fiona ordered in a firm voice. "Count to a million by tens. We're going to get you inside someplace nice and warm, then I'm going to run home for help."

She shifted his bulky weight onto her hip, swivelled her head and looked around. There must be someplace they could go to wait out of the rain. In the corner of the new subdivision, at the end of a row of cement foundations, she noticed a half-finished house with fresh tar paper on the walls and blue shingles on the roof.

"Stanley, run over and see if there's a way we can get into that empty house. Pretend you're an Indian scout and this is your first assignment."

Stanley shot off like an arrow, while Fiona

struggled to guide her brother towards the unfinished house.

Suddenly Everett's knees buckled. For a moment Fiona thought they were both going to end up in the muck, but she managed to shift his weight against her side and steady the two of them again. If only he'd stuck to that diet last January instead of foraging for food all day long like a bull moose.

"Don't quit now, Ev!" Fiona urged. "I told you to start counting. Every step gets you closer to a place where you can lie down and rest. Come on! You can do it. Ten, twenty . . . "

She watched Stanley gallop back in the steady drizzle. He slapped his hands on the legs of his wet jeans to make his imaginary horse go faster. "A window, a window, I found an open window," he sang as he bobbed past on his way to retrieve the wagon.

He was right. Peering through the rain–streaked unlatched window, Fiona saw a dry concrete basement where Everett and Stanley could wait while she ran home for help.

Everett counted quietly to himself, concentrating very hard on what came after three hundred and thirty when Fiona propped him up against the tar paper siding. "Will you be all right for a minute while I see if we can get in here?" she asked.

Everett looked dazed, but he nodded a yes and muttered, "three hundred and sixty . . . "

Stanley arrived with the mud-spattered wagon and bent down to watch Fiona slide through the window. Fiona hung by her arms from the ledge, feeling for the floor with her dangling rubber boots. She couldn't see how far she would have to drop, so she took a chance and let go, landing safe and sound a split second later.

"We gonna have a picnic in there, Fin?" asked Stanley.

"You bet, Mighty Mouse," she answered. "Now help Ev over here to the window and turn him around with his back facing me . . . just keep his foot out of the muck."

Everett was too shaken up to argue. Next thing Fiona knew, her brother's rear end had presented itself at the window.

"Now lower yourself down backwards, feet first, and I'll grab you before you hit the deck. There's a bit of a drop, but I'll catch you, don't worry."

Everett slowly eased his bulky weight down the wall with Fiona guiding him from below. He winced as she put out her knee to take his weight and keep his injured foot off the floor.

It worked like a charm. Within two

minutes Everett was sitting against the furnace in the middle of the dry cellar, counting past six hundred and eighty.

"You're next, Stanley," Fiona called, but it was the picnic hamper that dropped towards her as she looked up, clunking her hard on the head. Now two grubby boots inched over the window ledge and a soggy pair of jeans wriggled and dripped muddy water into Fiona's upturned face.

"You'll have to jump," she explained, spreading her arms to catch him.

"No way!" Stanley hollered. "I'm gonna fly!" He let go with his hands and flapped his arms, sinking like a rock and flattening Fiona in a heap on the hard floor.

Springing to his feet, Stanley shrugged off the wet poncho, then rummaged around in the overturned picnic hamper until he came up with his Batman flashlight. He flicked it on and shone the beam around the shadowy basement. "Let's betend we're in a robber's hideout, lookin' for treasure."

Fiona let him wander between the furnace and the hot-water heater, as he shone his Bat-beam to light his way in the semi-darkness. Fiona looked around. Piles of sawdust, a push broom and a few empty paint cans led to the only sign of life in their dungeon; under a wooden staircase, some workmen had left behind an empty paper bag and a black lunch bucket with a broken handle.

Stanley climbed up two steps, turned and jumped to the cement floor. Then he shone his flashlight beam and stomped up to the fourth step, and hopped down to the bottom again.

Fiona turned her attention to her brother who sat staring into space, looking scared and sick. "How you feelin', pal?" she asked, as she placed her hand on his forehead. Oh oh, she thought. Stone cold and clammy. Things were getting worse fast. Before he knew what she was doing, Fiona had gingerly lifted Everett's leg and slipped off his wet sock.

Everett bit his knuckle and sucked in his breath. "It's broken, isn't it?" he inquired in a small weak voice. He leaned his head back against the grey metal furnace while Fiona examined his bloody ankle and twisted foot. "Don't touch it! It hurts!" he cried out. Now that he had stopped counting, tears spilled out of his eyes.

"You're going to be fine," Fiona stammered over the loud beating of her heart. Dragging the picnic hamper closer, she reached inside for something to wrap around the foot to

keep it clean and dry. Hmnn. Two sandwiches, an apple, two oranges and a paper bag marked "Dessert Only." Finally, she found a wad of Kleenex then opened the brown bag to take out a treat.

"Here, Ev, snack time. Nibble on this while I wrap up your foot." She handed him a chocolate-coated cookie then bent over his foot. It looked puffy and swollen. Fiona could see blood oozing from a gash just above the ankle. Darn. Darn. Double darn. If only I had paid more attention to Brown Owl during the First Aid badge test, she thought. The foot did look broken, but there was nothing around to make a splint with, and anyway, by the grey colour of Everett's face, he might be suffering from shock. She HAD to get him home.

Fiona decided to act as if everything was under control to keep her brother from worrying even more. She switched tactics. "This isn't so bad, Ev," she said brightly. "Remember the time Grampa closed the car door on his ear? He bled polka dots all over the sidewalk, up the back steps and right across the kitchen floor to the sink. What a mess, remember? Naw, this isn't so bad."

But all Fiona had to do was look at her brother's glazed eyes, his white-washed face, swollen foot and the little pool of brownish purple blood spreading on his ankle to know that THAT was a lie. She had to get help . . . fast!

Fiona's eyes roamed to the open window. She imagined herself climbing up the wall, crawling out into the rain and running all the way home for Mom and the doctor.

Wait a minute, she thought suddenly. Climbing up the wall? Even if I stretch, I won't be able to reach up high enough to grab that window ledge. It must be six or seven feet from this floor. Oh my gosh! We can't get out that way! What will we do now?

Eight

The wind howled and rain ticked against the basement window, echoing through the dark and gloomy cellar. Suddenly a floorboard creaked overhead. Goose bumps burst out all over Fiona's skin. She held her breath in an effort to listen.

Mouse-like sounds scurried above; then Fiona heard a thump, a gravelly "Ouch!", a kicking noise and finally "Dumb wall!" What was Stanley doing upstairs?

Quickly Fiona shrugged off her quilted jacket and laid it over her brother, who was now slumped low and making tearful, snuffling noises. "You just rest," Fiona whispered, staring at his sad face. She flicked a cookie crumb from the corner of his mouth. "I'm going upstairs to find a way to get us out of here."

Fiona bounded up the basement steps two at a time. As she searched from room to room, she discovered a trail of footprints in the sawdust on the rough wooden floors, but no Stanley. The front door was locked with a big bolt that needed a key, and in the back entry hall was a crate marked DISHWASHER, so she couldn't even get near the door. Every window she checked was sealed shut with new putty and heavy tape.

Creeping up another staircase to the bedroom level, Fiona called, "Stanley, are you up here?"

A low beam of light flickered, then shone its way down the hallway as the world's smallest ghost tiptoed into view moaning, "Welcome to my haunted mansion. Booooo!"

"Listen, kiddo, we've got big troubles," Fiona confessed grimly.

"You gotta go to the baffroom too, huh?" Stanley replied, wriggling anxiously. He hopped from one foot to the other, then squeezed his blue-jeaned knees together, disappeared around the corner and slammed a door in Fiona's face.

She hurried into the other rooms, trying every window, but with no success. "There must be a way out!" she muttered.

The toilet flushed and Stanley appeared behind her. "Watcha lookin' for, Finny?"

"A window that opens, so we can get out to find a doctor for Everett. His foot's pretty bad." Worry spread over Stanley's little mud-streaked face.

He lifted his eyebrows and stuck out his chin. "Is it bleedin'?" Fiona nodded, then had to swallow hard to keep from crying.

In the unpainted bathroom, up high near the ceiling, was a small frosted window... their last chance. Fiona climbed onto the counter beside the sink and stretched up tall. With all her might, she tried to force the glass to slide open.

"I had a bleedin' nose once," declared Stanley, "and my best shirt got all yucky, and when my Gramma seed the blood spots she said 'I told you not to pick your nose in church,' but my dad jist taked me in the men's baffroom and we used up aaaall the paper towels, so a whole bunch of people at the wedding got mad 'cause nobody could dry their hands after the beception. Hey! You got it open!" He scrambled onto the counter top for a closer look.

"Well, it's part way open, anyway," said Fiona, as she stuck her head and one hand out the narrow opening. Directly below, just a couple of feet away, was a little roof over the back door porch. The rain and the wind had let up and in the distance, clumps of blue sky peeked through the rolling thunder clouds. On the other side of Banducci's orchard Fiona could see the school and the coloured roofs of Shannon Avenue.

"Lemme see," growled Stanley. Fiona set his flashlight on the counter and hauled him up to have a look. His kitchen-curtain cape smelled damp and musty as it hung down in her face. The window was jammed, only partway open. Fiona would never fit through that small space. But then she thought of another alternative.

"Listen, my friend," she said seriously, "we really ARE stuck in a true life adventure and you can help us save the day. See that pile of sand down there?"

Stanley craned his neck out further, rubbed his nose with the back of his hand and nodded yes.

"How would you like to parachute down into that soft sand and scamper off quick like a bunny for help?" As she set him back down on the counter top and brushed his muddy footprints off her jogging suit, Fiona crossed her fingers, hoping this plan would work. "Think you can do it, sport?"

"It's still rainin' and I aren't got my poncho on, so my cape might get all wet again. I better not." He pursed his lips and tried to whistle, but all that came out was a bubble of spit.

Then Fiona had a bright idea.

"See that tough guy in there?" she asked, pointing to the reflection of a scraggly-haired four-year-old in soggy, saggy clothes perched in front of the bathroom mirror. Stanley blinked and peered closer, wrenching his mouth into ugly positions, fascinated by the scary faces he was pulling.

Fiona leaned down and caught sight of her own reflection. She smoothed her wet hair, focused her eyes like a hypnotist and pronounced in a hushed, majestic tone, "You are the most courageous Superhero in all the world!"

Stanley's little mouth curved into a joyful smile. He pulled his shoulders back and straightened his curtain cape. "Yup, I are, aren't I?"

"I think I found you just in the nick of

time, Mister Superhero. Only the King of the Heroes will be able to escape from this prison. Only you can rescue us." Fiona could see he was completely wrapped up in the fantasy, so she delivered the clincher. "The Great Unicorn Wizard has given me this magic flying dust to sprinkle on your scarlet cape. Now you can fly like the wind and bring back someone to help our wounded soldier. Quickly! You are my one last chance to save him."

Stanley hitched up his baggy jeans and sniffed up a bubble from his left nostril.

"Ready?" Fiona asked hopefully.

Stanley smoothed his wet rumpled hair, and with a tight-lipped smile tried to wink at his own image in the mirror. "Ta daaa!" he trumpeted. "Soup-erman to the rescue!" And before he could change his mind, Fiona heaved him up and he scrambled through the opening, then straddled the windowsill.

"Turn around carefully so you face me and let yourself down slowly against the outside wall," Fiona ordered. She watched his little face pinch in concentration as he followed her instructions. "Can you feel around with your feet to find that little roof over the back door?" Fiona stretched up taller to see how he was doing. "That's it . . . you're almost there . . . good!"

Fiona hugged herself with happiness. They were almost home free! "OK big fella, jump into that sand pile and you're on your way."

Two blue eyes gazed up at her, then peered all the way to the ground, then up at her window perch again. "I don't wanna," he said matter-of-factly.

Darn! Fiona racked her brain for a solution to the problem while Stanley crouched on the tiny roof, unable to get back inside, but afraid to take the final leap to safety.

The rain had stopped now and the wind was only a whisper, but deep low clouds still rumbled overhead. A bright shaft of sunlight chased long shadows across the darkening ground. It was getting late.

Just then, Fiona's foot touched Stanley's flashlight on the counter. She picked it up and switched it on. "You there, Superman!" she called to the little figure below. "I've found your magic flashlight! Is it true what they say about the supernatural powers of this mighty weapon?"

Fiona aimed the plastic torch so the beam of light shone in the mini-hero's face. His frown changed to a confident glow. "Yup. Want me to show you?" he piped up, rising from his squat to stand like a diver ready for take-off.

"You are so brave and strong, O Magic Hero," Fiona called. "Fly to the earth and spread the news about our wounded soldier. Tell them we are locked in this dungeon and need help. I, Princess Philomena of the Unicorns, will see that you are rewarded handsomely. Begone, my hero."

Fiona stretched her arm out the window as far as she could and tossed the flashlight. As she watched it roll down the side of the sand pile, the corner of her eye caught a glimpse of flying flowers.

The next thing she knew, Superhero was dusting grit off his wet jeans with one hand and scrabbling around in the sand with the other for one half-buried rubber boot.

He picked up his magic flashlight and snapped her a salute. Then the little guy galloped off into the field, slapping his pant leg to gain speed and hollering at the top of his lungs, "Help! We got a wounded sojer in the new house!"

Fiona slid off the counter, fished a big handful of Kleenex from her pocket and wet it with tap water. Then she returned to the basement, fumbling in the darkness to feel her way for the furnace where she had left her brother. "I wish I'd kept that flashlight," she thought.

"Ow!" yelped Everett, as Fiona stepped on his outstretched hand.

"Sorry, Ev. I brought you some cool cloths for your forehead and something to clean your ankle. How you feeling?"

He flung aside the quilted jacket she had given him as a blanket and rubbed his sleepy eyes. "Rotten," he complained. "I want to go home."

Fiona clucked like a mother hen. "Now, Ev, we just have to stay put until Stanley comes back with Mom or Dad." She dabbed at his forehead with a wet tissue and tried to find his pulse. Fiona was just beginning to feel like the head nurse in a hospital when Everett switched back to his old bossy self. "Bug off, Fiddle-face. I don't need you fussing over me."

Fiona shrugged, reached into the picnic hamper and pulled out a huge red apple. "Want one?" As Everett crunched into the apple, Fiona leaned down to check his injury, but the cellar was so murky now, she could hardly see twelve inches in front of her face. It was spooky just sitting there in the dark on the cold clammy floor listening to someone chomping and slurping.

To pass the time, Fiona invented a story about two kids who were locked in a root cellar for three days and had to eat turnips until they were rescued.

Everett guffawed. "That's nothing. I once read about a scientist who was locked in his laboratory for three whole weeks and had nothing to eat but the phone book, and he got all the way to the X's before he was saved."

Everett's digital watch flashed 4:58, when Fiona's ears perked up to a new sound of muffled voices.

"Sshh!" she hissed. "What's that noise?" She heard two people outside, coming closer. Fiona jumped to her feet and started yelling. "Hey, we're down here! Help! HELP!"

A pair of large green gumboots appeared at the basement window, then a face bent down and opened into a sappy grin. "Well, lookie here," whined a familiar voice. "It's Stringbean Malloy."

Fiona couldn't believe her eyes and ears. "Bradley! Shane! What are you doing here?"

Bradley squatted and squinted to see her better, but Shane pushed him out of the way and hucked a mud ball right at Fiona's head.

Fiona ducked as the mud whizzed past her right shoulder.

Scampering out of range, Fiona heard her brother whisper, "Here. Use this." She felt a hard half-eaten apple drop into the palm of her hand. Tightening her grip, she wound up her throwing arm and heaved. Splat! Just below the basement window, an ugly blob of smashed apple guts stuck to the grey cement wall.

"Darn! I never should have dropped out of baseball," Fiona muttered.

She could see Shane's leather gloves packing another gooey mud ball, so Fiona dove behind the furnace for cover. But just as he reared back to throw it, she heard a commotion outside. She watched in wonder as Shane's two green gumboots levitated right up into the air. Shane had disappeared before her very eyes!

Just then Bradley's head was thrust into the window opening and Fiona could make out a man's hand on the scruff of Bradley's jacket collar. From above, a voice spiked with anger stammered, "Whatsa matta you? You crazy? Atsa kids in trouble down there!"

"Banducci!" gulped Everett. "Now we've really had it!"

They huddled together watching the

window and waiting. "Oh, Ev," Fiona moaned, "I can just hear the policeman in front of the judge . . . trespassing, breaking and entering in a strange house, kicking an adult . . . I don't think I could stand living on bread and water and sleeping in jail."

"Don't be so stupid, Fiona. They don't put children in jail."

"You're probably right," she sighed. "We'll just be cut off from television and grounded for two whole years."

While they worried and wondered, a grunting and scraping noise told them that something was happening outside. Two straight wooden legs edged through the narrow opening and inched down into the gloomy dungeon.

"It's an orchard ladder!" gasped Everett in amazement. "C'mon, let's get out of here."

As he struggled to his feet, Fiona lunged to steady him. At once, Everett leaned back against the furnace, fighting to catch his breath. A far-off look misted over his eyes, then his knees buckled. "Fiona, I don't feel so goo . . ."

Everett clutched his stomach, doubled over and promptly threw up.

Fiona flinched and turned her head away just in time to see the end of the ladder touch the cement floor. She turned back to her sick brother and tugged at his sleeve. As if he was in a slow motion replay, Everett pitched forward and crumpled in a heap at her feet.

"Oh no!" she cried. "Not now, Everett! We've almost made it. I can't lift you out by myself. You're just too heavy. Get up!"

"Ay girl! Why you wait? Climb ona ladder. We help you."

"I can't," Fiona called, biting back the tears. "My stupid brother fainted. Now we'll never get out."

Fiona tried to be brave, but with the sickly smell of thrown-up cookies and apple, Everett's motionless body slumped against her leg and the gathering gloom of their dark prison, she lost all hope.

Nine

Fiona sat down, wrapped her arms around her boney knees and rocked back and forth in misery. She felt like a music box ballerina that somebody kept forgetting to rewind ... so tired that even her thoughts were in slow motion. She wished she could just be home asleep in her own bed. Her bed? That was it! All they needed was a bed!

"Bradley, climb down here and help me lift Everett onto the end of the ladder," Fiona called excitedly. "We can use it like a stretcher, then Mr. Banducci and Shane can haul him up and out from the other end."

Soon they had hold of Everett's arms and legs, and together they laid him, stomach down, onto the rungs of the ladder which really did look like an old-fashioned hospital bed for a wounded soldier.

Outside, Mr. Banducci pulled while Shane leaned in through the window to guide the rest of the ladder over the ledge. Down below, Bradley and Fiona steadied their end, listening to the wooden ladder creak and scrape as it was dragged and pulled up and out.

"He's almost there!" Fiona shouted.

Suddenly the ladder snapped in two. A hand latched onto Everett's jacket and yanked him to safety just before three broken ladder slats clattered to the concrete floor.

Stanley shouted from outside. "We saved you, Ebret. Wake up!"

Fiona cupped her hands around her mouth and called up to the rescue party. "Just lay him in the wagon and take him to your place, Mr. Banducci! Get him to the doctor as quick as you can. Don't worry about us."

She turned to Bradley and offered her hand in friendship "Phew! I think the worst is over. Thanks, Brad. I couldn't have done that without your help."

Bradley's eyes narrowed like a jungle cat's. "If you think I'm spending all night in this freaky dark basement, you're nuts. Now, let's get out of here."

"Oops," Fiona said in a wee small voice. "There is no way out."

Bradley grabbed her by the scruff of her shirt and stammered, "Wha . . . what do you mean?"

Fiona gulped and frantically searched her brain for a solution. Suddenly she remembered the jammed window upstairs. "C'mon Bradley, follow me."

They bounded up the stairs two at a time. Fiona felt as light as a feather, relieved to know her brother was on his way to the doctor. He was going to be all right.

One minute later, she and Bradley were standing on the bathroom counter trying to force the sticky window to budge a few inches more. "Yes!" they shouted with glee, as the glass frame slid open wide.

Fiona bent over like a table and Bradley stood on her back to climb up and out. "Hurry up!" she ordered. "You weigh a ton! When you get all the way out, stand on that little roof and help me up."

Leaving scuff marks all the way up the wall, Bradley squeezed through and pulled himself over the window ledge and outside.

"My turn at last," sighed Fiona.

Bradley reached back inside and said, "C'mon Malloy. Gimme yer hands."

In no time at all, they were both outside, standing on the porch roof, waving to Mr. Banducci who was walking backwards through his orchard, pulling a heavy wagon load. Sprawled in Stanley's lap was Everett, struggling to sit up, but the little Superhero kept thumping him in the shoulder and knocking him back down again. Shane stumbled along beside the wagon, trying to keep up while holding Everett's bad leg high in the air. All the while Mr. Banducci kept barking at Shane in Italian.

Fiona couldn't help but laugh. "Bradley Newcomb, you are an OK guy," she said with a grin, pounding him hard on the back. "Www-wa-watch it," he quivered, eyeing the eight-foot drop to the ground. He inched cautiously away from the edge, steadied himself and squatted like a caged animal.

A light went on in Fiona's brain. "Don't tell me you're afraid of heights, Bradley?"

He grabbed her arm so tightly, Fiona thought it might break, then bit out mean angry words. "Don't you dare laugh at me, Malloy."

He shuddered for a moment, then rested his chin on his knees. "My dad was a glider pilot," he murmured, cracking his knuckles in short jerky motions. "He crashed and died last April. Something inside me just freezes when . . . " He shook his head as if it would help him erase the memory.

"I . . . I didn't know," Fiona said gently.

Bradley scraped his knuckle over his teeth and quietly continued, "My mom's still a basket case, working all day in the hotel and in the donut shop most nights." He hung his head and punched his fist into his leg.

"Gee, I'm sorry, Brad."

"Yeah, sure. Everybody's sorry."

A gust of wind sailed past them. Fiona sank to his side and hugged her knees to her chest. "I just didn't know."

"Nobody knows," Brad muttered bitterly. "And nobody cares. You try being the man of the house when you're eleven or twelve. Sometimes Shane and me just get so fed up we take off and . . . aw, forget it."

A hawk circled above the orchard in a graceful, gliding swoop. Brad leaned his head back and closed his eyes. "If I had wings, I'd

fly a million miles away and make up my own world," he said dreamily.

Fiona gave him a slow smile of understanding. "Bradley Newcomb, this may come as a surprise to you, but I have actually thought the EXACT same thing myself. So you see, we do have something in common."

They sat for a minute thinking their own private thoughts. It felt good to have made an enemy into a friend, but how could Fiona convince him it was safe to jump off the roof into that pile of sand? Far off in the distance, Fiona heard the 5:15 freight train rumble over the Flitton Bridge. Soon it would be dark. She couldn't leave Bradley up there all alone, but she wanted to go home. She had a science project to plan for Monday.

Then an idea burst in her imagination like a soap bubble.

"Yikes!" Fiona screamed, clambering to her feet. She brushed her hand frantically against Bradley's shoulder. "There's a horrible looking spider crawling up your back!"

Brad twisted his head to look. He jerked his shoulder, jumped to his feet and frantically flicked his hand behind him. Fiona slapped at the back of his jacket, then shoved him into mid-air and leaped. They were flying!

The next thing they knew, they were

sprawled on their backs in the sand pile, laughing like loons and spitting grit out of their teeth.

"You tricked me!" Brad said with a grin. He gained his balance and helped Fiona to her feet. "How'd you think of that? I couldn't figure how we'd ever get down."

"Well, Bradley, old buddy, old pal, it's easy when you have what my father calls a 'fertile imagination,'" Fiona laughed. "As a matter of fact, while we were up on that roof, I came up with an idea for a science project that will knock Mr. Johnson's socks off! Let me tell you about it while we head for home."

Ten

The next day was Sunday, but for the first time in her memory, Fiona and her mother did not attend church. Instead, they brought Everett home on crutches from a night in the hospital. Reverend Malloy arrived home from services just in time to carry the rocking chair into the kitchen and help Everett prop his cast on the footstool his grandmother had embroidered.

While their parents stood over the sink peeling a giant mound of onions and wiping their eyes, Fiona and Everett joined Stanley who was blowing on a steaming mug of hot chocolate. Everyone argued good-naturedly about who had rescued whom. Just then the telephone rang.

"I'll get it," said Fiona. She cradled the receiver by her ear and licked at the fringe of marshmallow on her upper lip.

"Hello. Oh, Mrs. Wong! How was business yesterday? Wow! Yes, they're peeling them right now for a big pot of soup for tonight's church supper. OK I'll tell her. Thanks again for calling."

Before she could say another word, the back doorbell rang. As Fiona held the door, her mouth flopped open like a cod fish.

There on the back porch stood Mr. Banducci with a big paper bag under his arm. Right behind him, struggling to lift a bushel basket of apples off the deck of a farm truck was Shane Newcomb. And right behind him was Bradley, propping Everett's bike against the garage wall.

Reverend Malloy's hand came to rest on Fiona's shoulder. "Don't just stand there gaping, Princess. Ask Mr. Banducci to come in. You too, boys." He held the door open as the Newcomb brothers lumbered past, setting the big basket of apples down on the speckled floor.

Bradley stuck out his chest. "Pretty heavy load, but we said we could handle it."

Mr. Banducci was all dressed up in a clean white shirt, white socks, shiny shoes and a pair of grey suit pants with navy suspenders.

"Won't you join us?" asked Mrs. Malloy, setting three more cups on the table and pointing to the bench seat under the calendar.

Mr. Banducci reached into the paper bag and pulled out a wreath of purple flowers. "First, I like a make a little presentation." He stepped towards Fiona and held out his hand. "For the little princess."

Fiona gulped down her surprise and stretched up proud and tall as two wrinkled hands gently placed a crown of crocuses on the bumps of her ponytails. Everyone clapped and cheered.

"You no scared to tell me I was wrong, even when we hadda big fight. You send for help when you brudda in a trouble. I like a say I'm sorry what I say before. Now I'm a say you pretty much good kid." A wide smile stretched all the way to her ears as Fiona waltzed down the hallway to admire her royal crown in the mirror.

When she returned to the kitchen, she thought her eyes were playing tricks on her. A glorious, magical black cloak with red satin lining was twirling in a circle like a whirling dervish. When it came to a stop, she could see it was Stanley inside.

"Lookit the cape he gived me! Lookit the inside part all red and shinin'! I could betend I'm Superman and everthing!"

Mr. Banducci's black eyes twinkled. "I think he maybe have more fun than me when I wear it to the opera longtime thirty-five years ago. You make a brave hero, boy. You gotta lotta spunk. I'm a like you."

It was a wonderful celebration. Mrs. Malloy made grilled cheese sandwiches and cut into one of the lemon pies she had baked for supper. When he had finished the last crumb of pie crust, Mr. Banducci leaned back from the table and rubbed his full stomach contentedly. He told the others that he had given the Newcomb brothers weekend jobs in the orchard to keep them out of trouble and to give them a little extra pocket money.

"Just like a grandchildren I never have," he said with a wink. "Maybe I take a boys help me catch fish inna river today." Bradley grinned and lifted his plate to his mouth, licking the last bit of lemon pie filling.

Shane frowned and clipped his brother on the back of the head. "Cut it out, ya slob!" he muttered, as he propelled Bradley towards the door, booting him in the seat of the pants to hurry him on his way. "Thank Mizz Malloy for the lunch, Brad." Shane turned and tipped his baseball cap to Fiona's parents. He grinned, stuck his hands in his pockets and backed towards the door until he bumped into the fridge. "Oops, Sorry. Gotta go. See ya." His red hair and even redder face disappeared out the door.

Just as Mr. Banducci stood up to leave, Bradley whispered something in Fiona's ear. He tried to tame his unruly mop of red hair, then shrugged his shoulders, stuck on his hat and waved. "Thanks again. See you," he said as he held the door open for the old man. "So, Mr. Banducci, I figure the faster we finish our chores, the more time we'll have for fishin', eh?"

A few minutes later, Stanley's mother came over to pick him up for a visit to his Gramma's. Fiona's parents began to clear the table and carry the plates to the sink.

The slats of the old chair creaked as Everett sat there rocking, staring straight into Fiona's eyes. "I guess with my foot bandaged up like this, you'd better take charge of building that rabbit hutch, eh Fin?"

Everett's parents looked at each other as if they couldn't believe what they had just heard.

Fiona raised her chin with pride and replied in a solemn tone, "Sorry, Everett. No can do. I've already got a partner and we've come up with a great project of our very own!"

Reverend and Mrs. Malloy stepped up behind Fiona and looked over her shoulder as she produced a two-page plan written in purple ink on bright green paper, with a unicorn drawn in the top righthand corner. They leaned over the back of her chair and read:

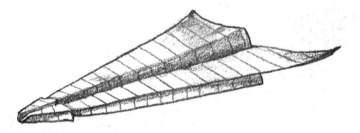

A Study of Aerodynamic Function in

the Design of Paper Airplanes

by

B. Newcomb and **F. Malloy**

Fiona's eyes shone with joy. "And you'll never guess what we've decided to call our fleet of experimental aircraft. Unicorn Air!"

Sandy Watson grew up with a sister and two brothers in an army family and attended eighteen schools throughout Canada and Europe. She now lives near Vancouver in the Surrey country-side where her two grown children come to visit. She teaches writing classes at community college and is currently at work on a new book about Fiona.

Terry Stafford's love of art took her to the California Institute of the Arts and the Beaux-Arts in Geneva, Switzerland. She wrote and illustrated her first four books for children, including *Matt and Jenny in Old Vancouver,* which earned the Canadian Children's Book Centre "Our Choice" award in 1986. Terry lives in Fort Langley with her husband and their three daughters.

Printed in Canada